I Live With Daddy

Judith Vigna

Albert Whitman & Company • Morton Grove, Illinois

Library of Congress Cataloging-in-Publication Data

Vigna, Judith.
I live with Daddy / written and illustrated by Judith Vigna.
p.   cm.
Summary: Olivia lives with just her dad since her parents got divorced. Now, even
though she has chosen to write a book about her mom's glamorous career as a TV
reporter, she manages to show that she loves both her mom and her dad equally.

ISBN 0-8075-3512-5
[1. Divorce–Fiction. 2. Mothers and daughters–Fiction.
3. Fathers and daughters–Fiction.] I. Title.
PZ7.V67Iaad   1997   96-32825
[E]–dc20
CIP   AC

To my Young Author friends at

Sacred Heart School, Bayside, New York,

and their teacher, Hermine McQuillan,

with love. — J.V.

Daddy and I live by ourselves. Last fall
he and Mom got a divorce, and Mom moved out.
I'm supposed to visit her apartment two weekends
a month, but my mom is a television reporter and
she works a lot, so I don't always get to go.

Mostly I see her on TV.

I miss my mother. Sometimes I think she left us because I did something bad. But Daddy tells me over and over the divorce wasn't my fault. He and Mom couldn't get along, no matter how hard they tried.

"But we both love you," he told me. "And we'll always take care of you. We promise."

Daddy cooks great pizza and fixes the hems on
the jeans Mom sends me. And I get to choose what
I wear to school, so long as Daddy's remembered
to put it in the wash.

We clean house together. He mops and vacuums
and gets the rings off the tub. I dust.

And he doesn't yell too much. Except once,
when I accidentally let the hamster out of his cage.
I yelled back, "Mom would have got me a dog!"
I thought he'd get angrier, but he just said,
"Who has time to walk a dog?"

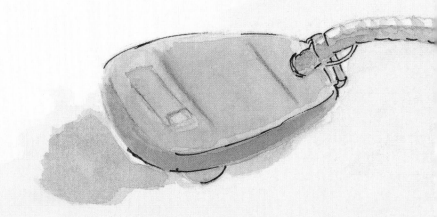

After school, I stay with our neighbor, Mrs.
Bronstein, until Daddy gets back from work. She
has a swing set, and when she pushes I can
almost kick the sky.

At home, I check for e-mail from my mom.
She tells me about the famous people she's met
and the great places she's seen.

... WITH THE PRESIDENT AT THE WHITE HOUSE .... INTERNATIONA

On President's Day Mom took me with her.
We flew in a plane to New York City.

There was a big television studio right
off the sidewalk. We could look through a window
and see celebrities being interviewed. While we
were watching, the singer Blanca Lee came out.
She said "Hi" to my mom. They had met on a
television show. Her driver took a picture of us,
and when it was dry she autographed it for me.

My mom's not as famous as Blanca Lee.
But the kids in my class think it's neat that she's
on TV.

So when we had to make a book for Writers'
Day, I decided to write about my mother.

Daddy helped me send e-mail to ask for some
pictures. And a few days later a package came
for me.

Mom had sent three photographs.

Her note said, "Dear Olivia, I hope these will
help. See you on Writers' Day. Love, Mom."

"Mom's coming!" I told Daddy. He looked
surprised. She almost never came to school.

The next day, I took the package to class.

Our teacher showed us how to make our own books. I pasted a picture of Mom on each page and made two drawings of how she looks on TV.

Then I wrote a story.

A television reporter tells the news. She knows everything that happens in the world. She gets to meet famous people. She is brave because she has to work in a tornado sometimes. This television reporter is my mom.

I called my book *Celia Beta Rollins for PNXT* because that's what she says on TV. My friend Ravi thought that was cool.

That night I asked Daddy to print out my story on his computer to make it look like a real book.

"I've got a lot to do," he said. "You'll have to wait."

But after supper, he helped me. We cut the computer printout into five strips, and I pasted one sentence under each picture.

I couldn't wait to show my book to my mom.

It was Writers' Day.

We all sat on the floor of the school library. Daddy sat in the back with the other grownups.

I looked around for my mom, but she hadn't come yet.

Then our teacher introduced a real live author. He showed us sketches and layouts from his books, and we got to ask questions.

Ravi wanted to know how old he was when he decided to become a writer. He said he was seven.

I asked him if he ever wrote about his family.

"No, but I usually dedicate my books to them," he told me.

The author finished speaking, and everyone
went to look at our books.

"Have you seen Mom?" I asked Daddy.

"No," he said. "Maybe she had to work."
When some parents asked me about her job,
he got a sad, funny look and went out to the hall
to get coffee.

People were starting to leave, and my mother
still hadn't come. She'd forgotten, I *knew* it.

Ravi saw how mad I was.

"You should have made your book about your dad," he said. "He comes to school all the time."

It was true. Daddy never missed anything, even if he had to leave work early. What if he thought I loved Mom more than him? What if he left me, the way Mom did?

Ravi tried to cheer me up. "You can make it up to him next Writers' Day," he told me.

"But that's a whole year from now!" I said.

Then I remembered what our guest author had told me. I could dedicate my book to someone!

Ravi helped me find a library book the author had written. "Do it like this," he said, pointing to the words in the front.

I wrote my dedication on the first page of my book, opposite Mom's picture. I snuck it in my book bag just before Daddy came looking for me. I wanted it to be a surprise.

Just as we were leaving, I heard someone call my name. It was my mother!

"I'm sorry I'm late, honey," she said. "There was a big warehouse fire, and I had to cover it."

While Daddy waited on the steps, I showed her my book.

"It's terrific," she said. "I'm so proud of you!"

"Can we go out for ice cream?" I asked her.

"I'm sorry, Olivia," Mom sighed. "Not today—I have to get back to the studio. But I just had to see my little author." She gave me a long hug. "You and I will do something special next weekend, I promise."

As my mother drove off, Daddy ran down to me.

"I wish Mom could've stayed," I told him.

He fixed my ponytail. "I'm sure she wanted to—she loves you very much."

Then he said, "I know how much you love her, too, and that's just fine with me."

I'm glad Mom remembered to come to school, anyway.

And I'm really glad I remembered Daddy.